Table of Contents

Chapter 1: A Meeting at High Technology

Troy looked at his phone for the third time in five minutes. Where were his brothers? They were supposed to be meeting in the conference room of High Technology in 10 minutes, but in his mind, early was on time and on time was late. This was an old holdover from his time in the military. Since his retirement, he has been running a multi-million-dollar tech company with his homeboys from back in the day.

Troy could hear Eric and Jamal coming down the hall laughing. "What the hell is so funny?" spat Troy, "The meeting starts in a few minutes."

"Cool it," said Jamal. "We are on time, and not CP time."

Both Eric and Jamal laughed while slapping each other's hands. They were brothers, so something as small as their differences of opinions around time was not going to come between them. When they were younger, Troy was always in charge. He left the hood and joined the military. He commanded his troops throughout his two-decade military career, and now he was trying to control Jamal and Eric and it was making them crazy! Troy towered over Jamel and Eric at 6 feet 2 inches with tone muscles that look like he was still in boot camp.

Jamal turned to look at Troy and said, "What is this meeting about? Ain't got all day to be here. I got places to go and people to see." Jamal was six feet and solidly built, with skin the color of coal. If he wasn't the Operations Manager at High Tech, he could be a bouncer at a club.

Troy was not surprised at Jamal's comment. He was always busy, sometimes doing things on the up and up and sometimes less so. "If you sit down and shut up, I will tell you, brother," Troy said calmly, using his training from the military to command the room and keep his temper under control.

Eric sat next to Jamal as Troy opened the meeting. He was the quiet one in the group. He was great with numbers, but not really a people person. If you were looking for him, the best places to start would be at his computer running numbers or playing his video games. Eric was tall and thin with a quiet assurance that made him look good.

"Today's meeting is about growth plans to expand the company," Troy started, "Kiera will be joining us in about 10 minutes to discuss some data insights."

Troy had to focus as he mentioned her name. He didn't understand the effect she had on him, but merely mentioning her name made his groin tighten. He hired her for her brain but noticed her beauty the first time he laid eyes on her in the interview. He was convinced that it was more than those attributes that caused his reactions to her. She captivated him in a way that no other woman had. But now was not the time to think about that; the company had to come first.

The next 10 minutes flew by and suddenly Kiera knocked on the door and stepped confidently into the room on 3-inch heels. She wore a knee-length black skirt that hugged her in all the right places and a pink blouse that showed a hint of cleavage. Her hair was in a loose bun on top of her head with a few wavy strands that accented her brown face and gold-speckled eyes.

Everyone rose from their seat as she entered the room, but Troy was the first to speak, "Thank you for joining us. Please have a seat."

Kiera sat to Troy's left, crossing her legs tightly to settle the shivers that ran through her body when she was near him. She didn't understand why her body reacted to him in this way. She had known and dated handsome guys in the past, but none elicited a reaction like Troy. However, he was her boss and nothing else. Nothing in his actions gave her cause to suspect that he wanted anything more than that. He was always professional and in control.

She shifted her attention across the table to Jamal and Eric and was met with looks of desire from them both. This suited her as she longed to be desired.

Jamal gave off a bad-boy vibe. He looked at her as if he would do all kinds of naughty things to her. Eric, on the other hand, looked like he would treat her like a delicate rose. She pulled her attention back to Troy as he concluded his part of the meeting before giving her the floor.

"I have reviewed the data and see that profits are forecasted to be 10 times what they were last year. We can use the profit to grow by acquiring additional businesses," Kiera began, confident that she knew her stuff. She could tell you where to put your money for maximum growth based on the research she did.

She had graduated from Spelman College with a Master's Degree in Computer and Information Science. She worked for a couple of tech companies before accepting a position at High Technology. She enjoyed working for the brothers. They respected her and never got out of line. She had heard that they behaved very differently in their personal lives. There were rumors that they had shared women in the past and wanted to be in a polyamorous relationship with one of the women they had all dated but she wasn't interested. Kiera liked all three guys and had feelings for each in different ways but she was at High Technology to be professional, not to hook up with her bosses. She dated a few guys in college, but they thought she was too independent and didn't need a man. While it was true that Kiera didn't need a man, it would be nice to have one.

Chapter 2: Threats and Fear

As the meeting was ending, Kiera's phone started to ring. "Hello, this is Kiera," she answered, her face blanked, "Why are you calling? Why are you doing this? Stop calling me!" Kiera hung up the phone.

The guys rushed around the table toward Kiera. "What's going on?" Troy asked, concerned.

"Someone has been calling and leaving threatening messages," Kiera explained, clearly shaken up.

Jamal took Kiera's phone and tried to dial the number back, but it was disconnected. Eric placed his hands gently on Kiera's shoulders to calm her.

Kiera looked down and said, "Last night someone threw a rock through my living room window with a note that said, 'die bitch.'"

"Kiera, why didn't you tell us about this? You know we can protect you!" Troy said, clearly trying to keep his cool but his anguish was evident.

"I-I," Kiera said. "I didn't want to worry you. It isn't your responsibility."

Eric embraced her, "We are a family here. We protect our own."

Kiera clenched her hands to her side. He stroked her back, trying to calm her down. His peaceful demeanor washed over her. She melted a little into his embrace.

"We need to find out who is calling you," Troy began as he launched into planning mode. "Jamal, do what you do to find out where these threats are coming from."

"You've got it, bro," Jamal said. "Don't worry Kiera, we will figure this out. You will be safe again. I just need your phone to do some research. Let me know if there is anything you don't want me to see and I can skip over that for you." Jamal reached out to take the phone from her, and their fingers brushed gently. Both of them paused for a moment.

Kiera sniffed, "Th-thank you all. I am sorry for all the trouble. Jamal, I don't have any secrets on my phone. Please do what you have to do."

Jamal quickly started to upload information from Kiera's phone onto his computer as Eric held her close. He tried not to think about the heat that he felt in his fingers as they touched for that brief moment. He had a task to do, and that was what required all of his attention.

Troy was thinking through various places Kiera could stay that would be safer than her home. Of course, his first thought was their brownstone because he would be nearby, strictly for security purposes, of course. He wondered if Kiera would object to staying at their place, she would probably worry about the implications of such a move, even if it was just for her safety.

Eric felt like the luckiest man alive, and he felt terrible about that. He had a beautiful girl in his arms and she was leaning on him for support, but she was only in his arms because something terrible was going on. He rubbed Kiera's back to keep her calm while his brothers worked on a plan. He had the most crucial role in all of this because of her proximity. He reminded himself that he couldn't make her uncomfortable.

The brothers were all working away at their piece of this insane puzzle that was just dumped in their laps when they all heard a loud noise that sounded like a bomb going off. Troy's military instincts kicked in and he tackled Eric and Kiera to the floor. The room filled with smoke and the walls shook.

"What the hell is going on?" shouted Troy.

"It looks like the office was attacked," Jamal shouted back. They must have planted explosives near the conference room.

Troy coughed as the room filled with smoke.

"Let's get out of here," Eric said, trying to be the voice of reason.

"Grab Kiera," Troy said calmly, back in control of the situation. "We have to get away from here quickly."

They made their way out of the conference room and out the back door, but they had no idea how close the attackers were and they needed to get away from the building before whoever did this realized that they had escaped. Thank goodness this was an after-hours meeting and everyone else had gone home.

Jamal looked up as he said, "I know a place in Florida. It will function as a great safe house."

Troy ran out first, ensuring that the coast was clear before he jumped into his black SUV, beckoning the other three to follow once he knew it was safe. Eric helped Kiera into the back seat, and Jamal quickly got in on the other side. They both felt better with Kiera between them so that they could shield her if anything came at them.

Troy focused on the road while Jamal made some calls and Eric focused on keeping Kiera calm. Driving in the city did not get you anywhere quickly and Troy was trying to stay focused on what their next steps would be as he turned the corner on their block and came to a dead stop.

Cops were surrounding the building. Something big must have happened while they were attacked at the office. This spelled trouble. Troy parked the car at the end of the block and told his brothers to keep Kiera safe.

He walked up to the nearest officer and asked, "What's going on? This is my home." Do you have a driver's license to verify your address? Troy took his license from his wallet and showed it to the officer. "Here you go," said Troy.

"We got a report of a robbery, sir. By the time we got here, the place was wrecked," the officer explained. "Do you think you can figure out if anything is missing?"

"I can take a quick look. We were just coming to grab a few things anyway. My brothers are in the black SUV down the block. I am concerned about the young lady's safety. Can one of the officers watch over her while we grab what we need and see if we can figure out what is missing?"

"Sure thing, sir. I will grab a couple of my men to protect her while you guys get what you need."

"Thanks. I just need to let my brothers know what is going on before anyone approaches the car. I know how they are," Troy said, still in command mode.

Troy and the officer took off in opposite directions to fill their respective men in on the situation.

After Troy told his brothers what was going on, they both let a string of expletives fly before remembering that Kiera was sitting between them, still shaken from the attack. They quickly calmed down and got out of the SUV, locking the doors, and greeting the officers.

They did a quick sweep of the house and grabbed the clothing that they needed, as well as a few other choice items. Troy noticed that some of his notebooks were gone as he went through the house, which was concerning, but he wrote all of his notes in code, so it was unlikely anyone would be able to decipher anything. Eric and Jamal noticed a few relatively innocuous items missing, but nothing major. This felt very odd to all of them. The robbery felt very personal, but none of them could figure out who would be out for them like this.

"Let's get to Kiera's house and hit the road, brothers. I need some space to think clearly," Troy said, hurt and appalled by the personal attack.

Everyone was somber on the short drive to Kiera's house. The car was silent until they turned onto her block, and she suddenly screamed in horror. Someone had broken her windows and spray-painted "get out of town" across her garage and front door. She was so frightened that she didn't want to stop. Troy took off down the road, ready to get Kiera and his brothers to the safe house.

Chapter 3: Off to Florida

Kiera was quiet for a long time as Troy navigated the freeway to get them as far from Atlanta as possible. Eric and Jamal were working on contacting the people they knew who might be able to help when she suddenly broke her silence, "Do you think this has anything to do with the man who keeps calling and threatening me?"

Troy responded, "I don't believe in coincidences, so it is highly likely. Try to relax. We will protect you, Kiera. We are here for you."

Kiera began to relax. She liked feeling protected. She shifted to get comfortable in the back seat of the SUV, but it was hard with two very large men sitting next to her. She couldn't move without touching one of them.

Eric made arrangements on his phone for the employees of High Technology to have some paid vacation time after coming up with a plan with Troy and Jamal. He then glanced up from his phone and noticed that Kiera still had on her four-inch heels. "Kiera, would you like a foot massage?"

She nodded, approvingly.

"Jamal, I am going to need a better angle for this. Do you mind if Kiera sits in your lap so I can ease her aching feet?"

Jamal tried to play it cool and shrugged as if he didn't care either way but he was ecstatic to have Kiera so close to him.

Eric guided both shoes off her feet, caressed her heels, and moved up, applying light pressure. Jamal enjoyed watching Eric massage Kiera's feet as she relaxed in his lap. His groin tightened with her on his lap and to see Kiera being taken care of was satisfying to him. The atmosphere in the car began to transform from tense fear to that of sexual tension.

Jamal leaned in to whisper in Kiera's ear, "You know, there is something that I have always wanted to do since the first time we met." Jamal leaned down and kissed the nape of her neck.

She let out a small moan and then turned to look at Jamal. There was a hungry look in his eyes that matched the desire in hers. He licked his lips and went in for a deep kiss. He first licked the edges of Kiera's mouth and then took the kiss deeper. Kiera's right foot slipped from Eric's lap as her legs opened slightly. Eric gently rubbed Kiera's leg while watching her and Jamal kiss. Eric moved his hand up Kiera's skirt. Her skin was soft and warm. He wanted more. He reached higher and higher up the skirt until he made it to her upper leg.

Kiera started panting and moaning. "I like this," Kiera said as she slid off of Jamal's lap so she was between them again, and she quickly resumed kissing Jamal.

Breaking from the kiss, Jamal said, "Open your legs a little wider for Eric."

She obliged. Eric slowly pressed his fingers against her silky panties. He liked the fact that she was wet for them. He slid his hand beneath the thin fabric to find her throbbing bud. Kiera began to shake and move closer to his touch. She wanted more. Unzipping Jamal's pants first and then Eric's, she glided her hands down their hard shafts. She wanted to let them know that she enjoyed what both men were doing.

Jamal trailed kisses down Kiera's neck. "Open your legs wider so Troy can see your wet pussy."

Troy looked in the mirror and saw Eric's fingers caressing Kiera. He licked his lips and moaned, "Y'all are torturing me here. If you aren't careful, I will have to find a hotel off this highway and join the party."

The scent of Kiera's excitement was intoxicating in the SUV. Eric slid one finger inside of her moist, tight pussy, followed by a second finger. "Yes," Kiera said as she rode his fingers. He buried his fingers to the hilt as her juices covered his hand. Kiera moaned loudly as he pumped and moved his fingers more and more.

"Let me help," Jamal said.

He rubbed her clit while Eric fingered her deeply. Kiera continued to massage the soft outer flesh that clung to the hard barrels of both men. Their bodies moved in unison. The men took turns kissing and playing with her until they felt her shaking as she screamed while climaxing. She had never had so many hands pleasure her at once, but she liked it.

They then erupted themselves as Kiera continued milking their pulsing cocks. She felt sated and went quickly to sleep. Jamal and Eric rested their heads on the back of the seat and wrapped their arms around her. Then they all dozed off as Troy drove to their destination.

Kiera's phone startled her awake. She saw her friend Jasmine's name, so she answered it.

"Hey girl what's going on? I just went by your house and it looks a mess. Where are you? Are you okay?" Jasmine questioned her rapidly. They had been friends for years and Jasmine was always there for her; whether it was late night wine and movie nights or helping Kiera get over a breakup. Jasmine was like a sister to her.

"Jasmine, it is so good to hear your voice. I am so sorry I didn't get a chance to call you. Someone vandalized my home and attacked the office. I think I have a stalker or worse."

"Oh, my word," yelled Jasmine, "are you safe?"

"Yes, I am with the guys from work. They are protecting me, and we are getting away so we can figure this all out and stay safe at the same time."

"Please stay safe," said Jasmine, "and I will look after things here. I miss you already my dear. Please keep me in the loop."

"I miss you, too! I will do my best to keep you informed, but communication may be limited because we don't know what or who we are dealing with. Troy may be able to set up a secure phone line, but that will take a few days while we are working out the rest of what is truly going on," Kiera said, trying to keep the fear from her voice. "Stay away from my house and the office. It isn't safe for you. I would hate to hear that anyone hurt you to get to me."

"Keke, I can take care of myself. You know that," Jasmine said exasperatedly.

"No, Jazz, this is bigger than anything we have dealt with before. Stay away. I mean it. You should probably get a hotel as well. I can send you money for it since this is all because of me."

"I don't need your money, Keke. But if it will make you feel better, I will find somewhere else to stay. I don't want you worrying about me while you are dealing with whatever this is," Jasmine reassured her.

Kiera's life had changed so much in the last few hours. Her home was vandalized, her job was attacked, and now she was headed to Florida with three men, two of which had recently rocked her world with their hands and lips. She was confused because none of them had ever approached her like that before. She had feelings for them, and it was evident by their actions and the way they looked at her that they had feelings for her, but she didn't know where this was going. She decided at that moment that she would take life by the horns and go with it. She would help the men figure out who was trying to kill her and move on from there. She hoped that they could stop whoever the person was before it was too late. She wanted to have a chance to enjoy this adventure.

Chapter 4: Safe House

Troy stopped the SUV in front of a modern home overlooking the ocean as his phone started to ring. "Who the hell is this?" Troy questioned in a frustrated voice.

"We want the information from Kiera," said the mystery caller. "We will give you three days or that bitch will die." As quickly as it began, the line went silent.

Troy looked around, then spoke in a measured tone, "They want information from Kiera. They said if she doesn't give them the information in three days, then she will die."

Kiera's face turned to stone and she looked as if she had the wind knocked out of her. She leaned against Jamal and Eric as they walked with her to the house, supporting her weight, and making sure she didn't pass out.

"We're safe here," Jamal said, "I know the guy who owns this place and he has the latest and most expensive security system available."

After making sure that Kiera was safe on the couch with Eric holding her, Jamal checked around the house securing doors and making sure everything was in place. Once that was complete and Kiera calmed down a little bit, Eric took Kiera to the bedroom in the middle of the house. "Kiera, please rest. Let us get some information and if we find anything, we will let you know. But you have been through an ordeal today and you may be going into shock. I will bring you some water in a moment," Eric said softly, helping her lay down.

Kiera let Eric help her however he wanted but it wasn't until he left the room to get the water he promised that she realized the only clothing she had was on her body. She had nothing to change into sleep and she was not going to get any rest if she kept her work clothes on.

Eric brought the water, a large shirt, and a dress that he found back to Kiera's room but he stopped in his tracks as he was stunned to see how beautiful she was sitting on the edge of the bed. While they had a challenging day, he was certainly not expecting that she would still look so beautiful. He tried not to stare at her damp body in the bath towel but looking at her made him want to continue what they started. He set the water down on the nightstand and gave the shirt and dress to Kiera. "Thank you, Eric. I didn't have anything to wear," said Kiera. Putting on the large shirt, Kiera said, "Can you sit with me for a little bit? I don't want to be alone right now."

"Of course," Eric said, removing his shoes and climbing onto the bed as he helped Kiera lay back, holding her close, and stroking her hair. He reveled in their closeness. He kept his clothes on to make sure that he wouldn't go too far with her. He had deep feelings for her but, above all, his mama raised him to be respectful.

***

The house was modern with sleek lines and contemporary furniture. It had everything they needed; food, shelter, and a security system that couldn't be breached. Troy entered the security control center, a room with computer monitors and all types of high-tech gear. He took inventory of what they had to work with as he waited for Jamal and Eric to meet him. Jamal was the next to arrive and he was ready to launch into action. He was furious that their home and office had been attacked in such a personal way. He felt violated.

"Where is Eric? He should be here by now. We have work to do," Troy said, trying to start a plan in his head.

Eric finally came downstairs and met his brothers in the security room.

"Nice of you to join us," Jamal said to Eric as he sat down.

"Kiera just fell asleep. She was upset and frightened. She didn't want to be alone," Eric explained, remaining calm as his brother stared at him.

It seemed a lifetime ago that they left the High Technology office worrying for their safety. So much had changed; their house was robbed, the office was attacked, and what a drive they had.

They sat around the table discussing various plans. They needed to figure out who was after them before they could jump into action. Troy used his connections at the FBI to run a scan on the companies that Kiera used to work for. Eric used his research skills to figure out who the phone call could have been from. Jamal called on his more nefarious contacts to see if they had any information that could help them figure out what was going on.

Everyone was hard at work doing their part when Eric looked at his brothers. "You know, I like Kiera," he said in a quiet but confident voice.

"I do too," Troy responded, still buried in his work.

"So, what should we do?" asked Jamal.

"I know this is not the best time to start something but maybe we should try a poly-relationship again," said Troy. "We would share her. She could be the one we need."

"I don't know," Jamal said. "It was too much for Julie. I don't know if I can get my heart broken again."

"But this is different," Troy explained in the way only he could, "It is clear that Kiera wants us all and we want her. She is smart, beautiful, and sexy as hell. She really does something to me."

"Me too," Eric and Jamal agreed in unison.

"Let's get to know her more and see where it goes from there," Troy said effectively before ending the conversation.

Chapter 5: An Empty House

It was getting late. Each of the brothers had exhausted their resources and were waiting to hear back from their boots on the ground. Their conversation stopped when Kiera wandered into the command center wrapped in the large shirt, causing all of the gentlemen to gape a little bit.

"I'm sorry to interrupt," Kiera said as she blushed at the attention she was getting from her bosses. "I just woke up and was kind of hungry, but I don't know what I can have from here and I am afraid to use my credit card in case whoever is out to get me has a flag on it somehow."

"You aren't interrupting anything. We were just saying that we were getting hungry and figuring out what we should do for dinner. It has been a while since any of us have eaten and it has been one hell of a day," Troy reassured her as he crossed the room to offer his embrace.

Jamal said, "Hey Eric, let's go get some food from the Jamaican restaurant I saw on the way here."

"Okay," said Eric and he grabbed the keys to the SUV.

"I will watch over Kiera," said Troy. "What would you like from the restaurant?"

"I think I will have some oxtails," Kiera responded as her stomach growled. The guys began to smile. We didn't take you for an oxtail kind of girl. She looked at them and laughed.

"Pick up some Jerk chicken for me," said Troy. "Did you see which bag I put the emergency cash in when we left?"

She looked at them and smiled, feeling a little bit better than they had even thought of her at all. She felt a tingle run through her fingertips as Jamal and Eric left. She was not sure what it meant, but she had a good feeling when Eric smiled at her. In the middle of this hell, there seemed to be a bright spot and it was coming from a most unexpected place.

"Would you like a drink Kiera?" Troy said as his brothers left.

"Yes, please," Kiera responded, getting used to Troy's closeness.

He led her by the hand into the open kitchen. "What would you like? We have water, soda, wine, or Don Julio."

"Oh, they all sound lovely. I will have whatever you are having," Kiera said.

Troy got two glasses down and filled them with Don Julio, handing one to Kiera and taking the other for himself. They made their way to the bar to wait for dinner to arrive. The house felt quiet with the other guys not around.

"So, tell me something about yourself, your hopes and dreams," Troy said, trying to take advantage of the alone time.

Kiera remained silent for a moment, thinking about how to respond, "Well, Troy, I always dreamt of having it all, the job, the family, the house with the white picket fence, and more. I have been in a couple of relationships in the past but there was something always missing."

"Did someone hurt you, Kiera?" Troy asked, feeling a hatred rising from within towards anyone who would dream of hurting the sweet young lady standing next to him.

"No, not really. Just a lot of disappointment. Growing up, I always wanted a family. My parents divorced when I was younger. My mom did the best she could, but I still wanted a father figure around. She worked hard and had multiple jobs to support us, so I had to stay with my grandmother. I would see happy families with a mother and father, and I wanted that. It just hasn't happened yet. I began to be hopeful when I joined your company. I finally had a job and a home, but now things are a mess." Kiera paused, "Enough about me. What about you?"

Troy embraced Kiera and pulled her tightly against him in a protective hug. "Well, you know I served in the military for 20 years. He gazed at her eyes. I did a couple of combat tours in Afghanistan and that really changes a person. I retired and started High Technology with my homeboys. We are close, they were there for me after I came back and my head wasn't quite right. They listened to me and helped me overcome that stuff that's why we are so close."

"From what I understand, very close," Kiera said with a smile, "I heard you share women," she continued matter of factly. "What is that all about?"

He shifted so he could look Kiera in the eye, grateful for the Don Julio in his glass. He responded in a gentle but measured way, "Yes, we have shared women in the past, but now what we are looking for is a family of support. There is no jealousy and everyone protects our queen. One day we would like to have a family that supports each other's dreams and raises children. Each child would have all three of us for support."

Kiera sat quietly for a moment, looking into Troy's eyes, searching for any hint of insincerity but she was unable to find any. She began to get lost in his eyes and his scent. He smelled of dark hickory wood and hard cider.

"Can I taste you?" asked Troy, bold as brass, as he pulled Kiera back into him.

"Taste me?" Kiera asked, suddenly very bashful. "Of course," said Kiera coyly.

Troy caressed her cheek before taking her lips, first slowly then more possessively. He licked and teased, starting with the corners, and moving toward the middle. He broke away from the kiss and Kiera looked disappointed, but he simply shifted their positions. He picked Kiera up and placed her on the bar, so he could have better access.

Troy looked into Kiera's dark but inviting eyes. "I don't know what it is about you Kiera, but from the moment I saw you, I wanted you. I wanted to touch you and make you moan with passion." "Troy, I felt a connection with you too," said Kiera.

He slowly and gently took off her t-shirt, exposing her beautiful body beneath. He liked the way her curves dipped and dived. He marveled at the way her brown skin gleaned. He liked the way her arousal smelled. He licked her body starting with her brown nipples. He kneaded one while sucking the other to a hard tip. Kiera stroked the front of Troy's pants. "Troy, I want you too." Lying her on top of the bar, he continued kissing down her smooth abs to the top of her mound. He removed the blue lacy garment, then continued kissing. First sucking her swollen bud, then filling her with his finger.

Kiera shook and pleaded for more, "Please Troy, I need this."

Troy was happy to keep going as he pumped his finger inside Kiera while sucking her bud further into his mouth. He loved the sweet taste of her. Guiding his finger in and out, Kiera screamed and released herself to him. Troy licked her like he was drowning in water. He stopped for a moment before sweeping her up into his arms and carrying her to the master bedroom. He laid Kiera on the bed, he looked in her eyes and could see the passion growing. Kiera looked on as he grabbed the condom and rolled it over his enlarged shaft.

"I want to make sure you are protected, in all ways," he said as he slid between her welcoming legs. Kiera could taste her essence as Troy kissed and sucked her tongue. His hands rubbed her legs and he gently caressed the junction between her thighs. He slowly guided two fingers into her wet opening. He stretched her with his fingers. She was so tight. "Open wider for me Kiera, I want to make it good for you."

She spread her legs and shifted her hips. He removed his fingers and plunged his hard shaft into her wet and waiting pussy. He began to rock, first slowly, and then faster and faster. He was panting and groaning. She felt so good around his cock. He hadn't had sex in a long time. He and his brothers focused all of their energy on building the business for the past few years. Since Julie broke up with them years ago, he hadn't had time to date. At some point, he stopped bothering to even look at women in that way. That is until Kiera showed up for her interview last fall. This was the moment he had been waiting for since that fateful day. He wasn't even sure how he got here, but he was going to enjoy it while it lasted.

Kiera moaned and cried out. He was touching her like no other. He pulled out, flipped her over gently, and positioned her on her knees before he plunged in deeper, as he rubbed the rosette of her bottom with his thumb, dipping it in as he felt Kiera begin to tense. It was obvious she was getting close to her climax as she screamed, moaned, and panted.

"Cum for me Kiera," said Troy, inviting her to join him as he climaxed deep within her. Their bodies became one as they rode the waves that washed through them. Afterward, he slid out, took off the condom, and cuddled her close.

Jamal and Eric got home and heard the sounds of passionate sex. They quietly walked toward the main bedroom and looked on from the doorway. They loved seeing Kiera in the throes of passion. They all wanted to make her happy. Before their presence was noticed, they went back to the living room to layout dinner and wait for them to appear.

When they emerged from the room, Kiera and Troy were hungrier than before. "Let's go eat," Troy said, trying to remain cool. Troy and Kiera walked into the living room to join the other guys. Everyone grabbed their food and started eating and watching TV. They were like a family with their flower Kiera in the middle.

They were enjoying a movie on Netflix when Troy's phone rang. "We have information on who could be doing this," the caller said, following up on their earlier conversation with Troy. "I think it could be someone from Mid Tech. Kiera must have uncovered some damaging information about their security system and known breaches. They don't want the information to get out and will do anything to keep this information out of the public eye, even kill for it."

"So, what's the plan?" asked Troy.

"We will question the people from Mid Tech and get back with you. Ask Kiera what she may know so we can get to the bottom of this."

Chapter 6: The Long Drive

"Kiera, Agent Louis mentioned that this may be the work of someone from Mid Tech. Did you work there in the past and have information about data breaches or other important security information?"

Kiera's face fell. "Now that you mention it, I did. I told them that their clients' data wasn't secure. I even shared the holes in the system. They didn't want to know, so I hid the information on a shared drive in a post office safety deposit box. I was always taught to cover your tail when working in IT."

"They want the information back or they will hurt or possibly kill you. This information, if released, will cost them millions of dollars," Troy said somberly.

"But I can't get access to the post office box. It's back near my home!" Kiera said, panicking. "They are going to find me and kill me! Now all of you are at risk too! I need to go away. I need to put as much distance between me and all of you as possible. I could never live with myself if any of you got hurt or killed over my past!" Kiera began to cry.

"Don't worry," said Jamal. It was his turn to wrap his arms around her, calming her down. "I know a guy who works at the post office. He can probably access your safety deposit box. Please breathe for me. I can't have you hyperventilating while we are trying to make plans."

Now that they had some solid leads that they could act on, the guys began planning how to get the information, and fast! They had heard about the guy who ran Mid Tech and none of it was good. Troy did not believe in corporate espionage but things still had a way of getting back to him. He wondered how Kiera managed to get away with the security information at all, let alone hide it from him for six months. Troy was battle-tested and was not going down without a fight. He was sure that this was shaping up to be one for the record books.

Jamal reached out to his friend from the post office and decided that he had to be relatively vague on the phone. He knew that his phone was secure, but he was not about to take any chances with Kiera's life. He and Kiera were set to meet him at a secure meeting place where Jamal had done some other deals. It was about a three-hour drive, but this would give Jamal the time he needed with Kiera. They would have to leave early, so he turned in for the night after he got off the phone. He needed to be sharp, especially since he wouldn't have his brothers to guard his back.

"Oh, before I go to bed," Eric said sweetly, "we picked up some clothes for you, Kiera. I hope you like them and they fit okay. It has been a while since I shopped for women's clothes, so I had to guess a little bit." Kiera took the bag of clothing and sat in stunned silence. Nobody had ever done something so nice for her. She had planned to wear her clothing from that morning on their excursion tomorrow, but this was so much better.

The bag was full of a mix of comfortable loungewear and more professional looking garments. They felt exquisite and expensive. She didn't recognize the brand, which worried her a little bit. "*How much did they spend on this stuff?*" she wondered, feeling guilty. They were in this situation because of her and all three of the brothers were treating her so well and being so kind. She excused herself, telling Troy and Eric that she needed to get some sleep as well, before hugging them one more time.

She made her way to her bedroom with her new clothes. She closed the door and sank down to the floor.

"What am I doing? These are my bosses. I shouldn't accept these gifts from them. It will change everything." She shook the thought out of her head. *"Everything had already changed. In the last 16 hours, I have had them all one way or another and they all had me as well."* But really what does this mean? I know that they must have feelings for more but could there be more?

After sitting with that thought for a while, she finally dragged herself off of the floor and into bed. Her mind was racing but, as soon as her head hit the pillow, the day's events finally set in and she felt absolutely exhausted despite her nap. Within minutes she fell into a restless sleep.

Morning came early as Kiera awoke in a strange bed in an unfamiliar room. As she sat up, the previous day's events rushed back to her, and what she and Jamal were about to do weighed heavily on her shoulders. She needed a shower before she faced anyone, let alone her bosses. She snuck out into the hallway, making her way to the bathroom before anyone noticed she was awake. She was relieved when she saw that it was already stocked with body wash and hair care products. She was not ready to ask Troy or Jamal, let alone Eric, where such personal items were hidden.

She figured out the taps in the unfamiliar shower and stepped in, enjoying the feeling of the hot water washing away some of her tension. She took extra care to make sure all of her most intimate areas were clean because she had no idea where the events of the day would take her. Finally, she resigned herself to face the men who had made it their mission to protect her. She wrapped a plush towel around her wet body and went back to her room to decide what she was going to wear, choosing from the outfits the guys picked out for her.

***

Troy, Eric, and Jamal sat around the island in the kitchen, sipping their coffee, and discussing their plans for the day. They had all woken up when Kiera started the shower, but they were giving her whatever space she needed to feel safe and comfortable. None of them wanted to mess this up. While Jamal and Kiera were out, Eric and Troy had to figure out who from Mid Tech was calling and how to end this without anyone getting hurt.

Kiera finally came downstairs in a purple dress that accented her eyes and skin in the most alluring way. "Oh," she said shyly, "I didn't realize everyone was already awake."

"Not to worry, sweetheart. We were just discussing how to stay productive while you and Jamal are out," Eric said. "What can I grab for you for breakfast? Coffee? Tea? Toast?"

"I am not hungry right now, but tea sounds nice, thank you," Kiera said as she sat on the last vacant stool.

Eric made some peppermint tea, knowing that it was Kiera's favorite because of its calming properties. She gratefully took the mug from him and sat quietly as the brothers continued discussing their plans.

"Alright, my brothers. It is time for Kiera and me to hit the road, said Jamal.

I have the secure line patched into my phone and Kiera will be leaving her phone here just in case she gets another call. I have already set up the software to trace any call that comes in as soon as it is answered. I will just need to upload it to the system so I can work on it," Eric explained.

Jamal shifted his attention to Kiera and said, "You might want to grab a snack. If we stop, we will be even more vulnerable, so I plan to drive straight to the secure location to meet my friend." He noticed the trepidation in her eyes. "I will keep you safe, but I am not willing to take any unnecessary risks."

Jamal and Kiera first drove in silence, which was weird because Jamal was always talking.

"Jamal, why are you so quiet today?" Kiera asked.

"I got a lot on my mind," Jamal responded shortly.

"Like what?"

"Like trying to keep your ass safe." Jamal didn't know why he was being so short with her, but he couldn't stop himself.

"Oh, is that all?" Joked Kiera.

"Yes," Jamal said, beginning to let her in, "I don't think you understand what you mean to us. What you mean to me. I know I put on this hard front, but, baby girl, this is driving me crazy to see you in danger."

"I didn't know you felt like that, Jamal." Kiera gently caressed Jamal's arm.

"Now, that's what I like," said Jamal, enjoying the way her fingers danced over his skin.

Kiera lifted his hand from the console and kissed it gently. They fell into comfortable banter, learning more about each other while Jamal drove. She played with his free hand for the rest of the ride, while he talked. She loved how close they were and wanted more. Their carefree talk did ease her worries about what they were on their way to do. She did not know who this friend of Jamal's was, and she was literally putting her life in his hands. She put on a brave face, but Jamal wasn't fooled for a moment. He knew that she was scared. If he was honest, so was he.

They met the man from the post office and took the package without incident. Clearly, he was used to Jamal operating in secrecy and knew that it was better not to ask.

"Let's get this back to the house," Jamal said quietly, as they made their way back to the SUV.

The drive back was relatively quiet, there was a sense of relief that washed over Kiera knowing that she had the information that Mid Tech wanted so they could plan from there.

Jamal broke the silence, "I want to take you somewhere." It was starting to get late. The sun was about to go down. Jamal pulled the SUV into the beach area. "We need to stop and eat. I picked up some chicken wings, potato salad, and drinks."

Jamal laid a blanket on the private beach area and laid the food out. Kiera and Jamal ate as they watched the sunset over blue water. Afterward, they laid and basked in the beauty of the day. Kiera, feeling bold, straddled Jamal. She then started grinding on top of him while on the picnic blanket. The breeze lightly touched skin while they were kissing. Kiera broke the kiss and stood up, showing Jamal her figure.

Jamal asked, "Baby girl are you sure?"

"Yes," said Kiera as she took off her dress, letting it fall to her feet. Dropping to her knees, Kiera crawled to Jamal and unzipped his pants, and pulled them down his legs. She removed Jamal's thick shaft while he looked on with a smile. Kiera seductively licked her lips then she licked the little white bead that arose from Jamal's cock. He tasted like citrus.

"Hmm," she said. Kiera played with the tip. She went deeper and deeper all while thrusting her hand back and forth. She hollowed her mouth and breath through her nose so she could take him even deeper.

"Baby girl I won't last like this, and I want to be inside of you," Jamal said, groaning.

Kiera grabbed the condom out of the picnic basket and slid it over Jamal's cock. Then lower herself. With Jamal, she felt free, bold, and darning. She rode him hard and fast. He pulled her hair, forcing her breast to his mouth so he could suck her nipples.

"Ride that dick, Kiera," shouted Jamal in between licking her hard-taut nipples. "Now cum for me, baby."

Kiera screamed as she and Jamal released their inhibitions. Jamal held Kiera as she straddled him. He didn't want to let her go, not now, not ever.

It was dark by the time Jamal started packing up their picnic. He didn't want to leave the serenity of their beach, but there was still business to be taken care of and they had taken a considerable risk stopping for so long. Troy would never let him hear the end of it.

Chapter 7: Overnight Watch

Eric and Troy were talking about increasing their network security for High Technology and would talk with Jamal about adding surveillance equipment outside as well. Jamal and Kiera returned to the house and found the guys on the couch talking and watching football. As soon as Kiera put her bag down, Troy's cell went off. The display showed "Unknown Caller."

"Put it on speaker," said Jamal, "it might be them."

"Did you get the present I left you?" the man on the phone asked.

"Who the fuck is this?" Jamal responded.

"Don't worry about names. Check the front door," he said in a menacing tone.

Eric went to the front door. Laying there was a dead deer. Kiera cried in disbelief.

"Next time this will be Kiera if I don't get that information," the caller said before the call disconnected.

"That motherfucker!" shouted Jamal.

"We have to stay calm," said Troy. "Getting upset and acting rashly will only end up with someone getting hurt. We need to keep our eyes on the cameras 24 hours a day. Eric, you up to take the first shift?"

"You know it, brother!" Eric responded before heading to the command center.

Jamal and Troy looked at Kiera. She was clearly shaken. Neither of them thought it was wise to leave her alone other than for the obvious need for privacy in the bathroom.

"Kiera, I think you will be safer sleeping in one of our rooms tonight. I am worried about you. You have been through so much in the past two days and I would feel better if I could keep my eye on you," Troy said, trying not to scare her while still expressing the seriousness of the situation.

Kiera agreed, barely knowing what she was agreeing to as the events of the day played on her mind. It was late, and she followed Troy to his room after grabbing some pajamas from the bag Eric handed her last night.

"Please get some sleep, Angel. I will be right here watching over you. You will be safe, I promise," Troy said, kissing her forehead.

Troy had his laptop in his room and continued to work late into the night while Kiera slept. He grew hard seeing her soft, delicate form in his bed, but now was not the time for that. He ignored his desire and continued to work on the plan to make sure everyone got out of this alive and in one piece. He knew Jamal was pissed, and if they didn't act soon, he would make some really bad decisions.

Around 1:30 a.m., Troy finally crawled into bed, cuddling Kiera close. She had been very restless as she slept. He hoped his presence would calm her. He drifted off to sleep and dreamed about the days that would come after this whole disaster was behind them.

Kiera woke up in Troy's arms. The clock said it was 4:13 a.m. *"Damn,"* she thought, *"why am I awake so early?"* She carefully slipped out of Troy's grip and went to the computer room to see Eric.

"Hi Kiera," Eric said before she entered the room.

"How did you know I was here?" Kiera asked, caught off guard by his greeting.

"I can sense your presence," Eric responded simply, not looking up from his work.

Kiera walked into the room with a two-piece teddy on. Eric finally finished what he was working on and looked up. She looked like an angel to Eric.

"I couldn't sleep and didn't know where else to go," Kiera said.

"You can watch the camera with me for a little while if you like," said Eric. He was the quiet one and that is what Kiera needed now. She sat down in the chair to his left, staring at all of the security footage in front of them. Eric turned Kiera's chair around to face him, "You know we will keep you safe and get this jerk."

"I hope so and soon," said Kiera.

"You are so important to us, especially me. Kiera, you are the one who truly sees me. besides by boys. I know I am quiet and shy, but you always find a way to bring me out of my shell."

Eric looked Kiera in the eyes and shyly asked, "May I kiss you?"

Kiera was caught off guard after what had transpired on the way down to the safe house, but she simply said, "It would be my pleasure."

Eric lightly kissed Kiera: it made her skin sizzle. They both stood and kissed more. "Kiera, I need you," Eric said.

"You can have me," said Kiera, deepening the kiss.

"Do you trust me, Kiera?" said Eric.

"Of course, I do. I wouldn't be alive if it weren't for you and your brothers!" Kiera said indignantly.

Eric led Kiera to a chair. "Please sit," he said. He grabbed a tie from the box and blindfolded Kiera. "Stay still," he said softly in her ear. Kiera shivered with anticipation.

She liked the way Eric took control. The inability to see heighten her other senses. She was reeling. Every touch elicited a reaction, every lick went deeper. He was not only touching her body, but he was touching her soul. She felt her hands being tied behind her. She was surprised at first and wasn't sure she wanted to give up so much control, but as his practiced fingers worked, she felt any fear she had slipped away. She felt him caressing her breast through the soft fabric. He started with slow circles at first. Then he released her shapely globes from the teddy, sucking and then nibbling before he scraped his teeth across her tender mounds. The pain and the pleasure were beyond anything that Kiera had felt before. She had never explored any type of kinky sex because it required a lot of trust and compatibility that she never found with her previous boyfriends.

Eric went to his knees in front of Kiera. Opening her legs, he sampled the moisture with his tongue. Mmmm, Kiera you taste so sweet, said Eric. He spread her legs wider so he could have better access. Kiera reacted instantly to the attention, moaning quietly at first before she felt a tingle in her belly, and she began moaning louder by the moment.

"Cum for me, Kiera," Eric demanded. He stuck his tongue deep inside her and thrust in and out.

Kiera screamed and bucked as Eric massaged her clit to wring every drop from her. He untied her and positioned her over the computer desk. She stroked his cock from behind, she wanted more. Eric grabbed a condom from the desk drawer, shielding himself and protecting her. He couldn't wait any longer. With his cock stretched tightly, he placed his hands on her hips and slid inside of her waiting pussy. He pounded relentlessly as if his world depended on it. His shyness slipped away as he continued pounding. He pounded away fear and he pounded away anything that would separate him from Kiera. Then they came together. Breathless and motionless they stood holding each other.

Eric slid out of her and removed the condom before lifting Kiera onto his lap, holding her close as they both came down from their explosive orgasms. He stroked her hair and kissed her forehead. "You were amazing, sweetheart," he whispered in her ear. "Thank you for trusting me."

Kiera smiled and cuddled closer to Eric before beginning to speak. "I must confess, I have never been tied up before. I felt so helpless when you blindfolded me but in the best way, like I knew you were the only one who would touch me but I couldn't control anything."

"I feel honored that you shared this experience with me, but it is late and I think you should get a few more hours of sleep."

"Troy would probably lose his shit if he woke up and I was gone," Kiera said pensively. "I have never seen him so worried before."

Eric laughed. "He absolutely would. You are right. Let's not give him a coronary and get your cute little butt back to his waiting arms."

Kiera returned to Troy's bedroom and slid back into his waiting arms. Although he seemed to be asleep, he gripped her closer, shifting to make sure his entire body blocked her from any harm.

Chapter 8: United in Pleasure

The next day Kiera woke with hope, she had found three guys that wanted to protect and support her dreams. *"But did they love her?"* She wondered. She wanted them to love her, protect her, and have a family. Maybe it wouldn't be the conventional family that she dreamed of but she would have a family. She had fallen for all of them. Each man was unique but willing to show her that they cared.

But Kiera couldn't think about love yet. Her life was still being threatened and everything was a mess around her. Mid Tech would send someone to kill her if they didn't give them the information they wanted. She decided that she would give them the information but wanted them to pay for the threats and attacks, so she came up with a plan of her own.

Troy was already awake and had left the room by the time Kiera got out of bed. She headed toward the shower. Getting in, she let the warm water and soap slide down her smooth curves. She finished her shower and wrapped a fluffy towel around her body to catch the remaining droplets of water. She went to her room and sat at the edge of her bed, daydreaming. She snapped out of her dream and quickly grabbed some clothes as she could hear the men coming toward her room.

"Kiera, do you have a moment to talk?" Troy asked in a kind voice.

"Of course, I do, Troy," she responded. "Come on in." Kiera sat on the bed as the brothers gathered around her.

Troy started to speak, "They want the information, Kiera, and we have to give it to them."

"I know," said Kiera, "but I also want them to pay for the pain and hurt that they have caused me." Kiera was strong, she wouldn't give the documents without a fight. She explained the rudimentary plan she came up with that morning and allowed Troy to make it into a workable solution that would keep all involved as safe as possible.

Kiera liked having all of them in the same room together. She got up and gave each of them a kiss starting with Eric. The current in the room changed from electrically charged to sexually charged. Troy pulled Kiera on top of himself as they continued to kiss. Jamal and Eric looked on. They all needed to be together.

Releasing her from the kiss, Troy said, "Kiera we all want you bad. Are you ready for something like that?"

"Yes, I want and need you all," Kiera responded enthusiastically. She felt bold and daring. She knew that a lot was going on and maybe this wouldn't last but she would enjoy the moment.

Standing, Troy took off his shirt revealing a toned six-pack with abs so lean that they rippled. Kiera unbuttoned his pants and they dropped to the floor. Kiera backed Troy up to the bed and straddled him while Jamal and Eric undressed. Troy pulled off Kiera's clothes, all while kissing her up and down.

"You taste so damn good," said Troy.

Jamal and Eric approached Kiera. Each grazing a nipple as they sucked and licked sending sparks straight to her pussy. Everyone took their time and reveled in the moment. They all kissed, sucked, and licked Kiera. Kiera licked and kissed Troy, then Jamal, and Eric.

Her temperature began to rise. "I want all of you inside of me," Kiera said confidently as she arched her back and slid on top of Troy's cock. He gasped at how tight Kiera was and clung to her mouth.

Eric positioned himself close to her right side. She stroked his cock, then replaced her hand with her mouth. Eric grabbed her hair so he could work her mouth up and down. Kiera moaned loudly, as she grinded on Troy and her mouth worked Eric.

"Take me deeper, take more of me," commanded Eric.

Kiera obliged, hollowing her jaw, and breathed out her nose so she could take Eric deeper. Her mouth was so full, as was her pussy. She didn't want anyone to feel left out, so she beckoned Jamal over, starting to stroke his hard cock.

Jamal grabbed the lube and asked, "Kiera, have you been penetrated here?" He touched between the junction of her round buttocks.

"No," said Kiera.

Jamal didn't want to cause her any pain. "Kiera there will be pressure at first but then it will subside and all you will feel is pleasure," he explained before parting her cheeks. Kiera felt something cold on the ring of her back entrance. "Kiera, push out," said Jamal, as he worked his long cock into the untried rosette of Kiera.

At first, she grimaced at the pain but moving up and down on Troy caused it to subside. Jamal was almost inside Kiera. "Let me in, baby girl," he said, "arch your back." Finally, with a groan, Jamal squeezed inside. You are so tight baby girl, said Jamal.

Kiera was filled. She was complete. She found a rhythm as she worked her mouth on Eric. She moved up and down on Troy's cock, arching her back to move with Jamal as well. Kiera moaned and she could sense something inside of her about to break loose. She wanted to ride the wave of ecstasy.

"I won't last long," Jamal said as he guided his cock in and out of Kiera's ass.

"Me neither," said Eric as he worked his dick in and out of Kiera's mouth.

Troy pumped Kiera from underneath. "Kiera, cum for us first," said Troy, as he thumbed her little tight clit. She whimpered then let out a loud shout as their bodies fused and they erupted immediately after her. They poured everything they had into Kiera.

They disentangled their bodies and curled up with Kiera in the middle of the pile on the oversized California King bed. The men quickly drifted off to sleep. Kiera was in her happy place, surrounded by three men who wanted to protect her. They may even have feelings for her. She settled in and drifted off to sleep shortly after the brothers.

Chapter 9: It All Boils Over

Pop! Pop! Pop! Bang. Gunshots could be heard outside.

"Get on the floor," shouted Jamal, "they must be coming for the information or coming to kill us all."

Troy slid Kiera to the ground and underneath the bed. Eric slid to the floor beside them.

"What's the plan, Troy?" asked Jamal, as a bullet flew past his ear.

"We have to get the shooter," Troy began, "There is a gun in the next room."

"I can get it," said Jamal.

"Next to it are the bulletproof vests, grab one for yourself and chuck the others in here so I can protect everyone," Troy commanded.

Crouching down to the floor, Jamal ran to the other room to retrieve the gun. Shots rang out in the house. Then there was a loud thud.

"They are coming into the house!" shouted Kiera.

"Let's go," said Troy as he, Eric, and Kiera left her bedroom to go to the command center to see where the men in the house were. Troy was hoping that they could get across the house without running into them, but he wasn't too optimistic. He just couldn't let Kiera know that because she trusted him.

"Don't move or I will shoot," someone said in a low, deep voice. "Give me the information." Two more men with guns came into view. "I said give me the information or I will kill the girl." The men pointed the guns at Kiera and Troy.

"You don't want to do that," said Troy.

"Give us the information or we will shoot."

"Okay," said Troy, "the information is in the command center in the safe. Let us take you there and you can get the documents and leave."

"Show us the way and no funny business or the bitch will get it."

Troy led the group, Eric brought up the rear, and Kiera was stuck in the middle. She was shaken to the core. She was quiet because she didn't want to make the wrong move. As they neared the hall to the command center, Troy noticed that Jamal was close. He quickly attacked one of the gunmen knocking him out while Jamal shot the second gunman in the chest.

Both men laid on the floor unconscious. Eric had the ringleader in a chokehold.

"Put him out of our misery," Jamal spat.

Eric tightened the hold just enough to leave the scumbag in a heap with the others.

Troy was pissed at himself for letting his guard down. Someone should have been watching the security cameras. He knew this was going to happen sooner or later. *"Hopefully, Kiera doesn't hate us for letting these guys get so close. She must be scared out of her skull."* He had to do damage control if he had any hope of keeping her in his life. She was so good for him and his brothers. He would have to figure it out.

Eric noticed that Kiera was in shock. He immediately picked her up and brought her to the couch. He covered her in a blanket and held her close. "Jamal, bring me some water," Eric said in a calm, even voice.

"You got it, bro," Jamal said, moving slowly to avoid startling Kiera any more than she already had been. He handed the glass to Eric and settled in on the other side of the couch.

Troy was in the command center, reaching out to Agent Louis and his other contacts that he had spoken to in the past few days. He needed to get them up to speed before the cops showed up. He was just wrapping up his last call as he heard sirens approaching. The police, fire department, emergency services, and the FBI arrived on the scene.

Troy approached the officer nearest to him with his hands raised. "I am staying in this house. It belongs to a friend of my brother. Three gunmen attacked us and threatened to kill us. My two brothers and our girlfriend are inside. We have subdued the assailants, and unfortunately, we had to shoot one of them to protect ourselves and the young lady they were after. Please enter the house slowly. Miss Kiera is already in a state of shock. I would rather like to avoid scaring her any further."

"Are you sure that the house is safe?" The officer asked, concerned for his men's safety.

"Yes, sir. The assailants are unconscious, and the gun that was used is in the kitchen, far from everyone in the house."

"Alright," the officer said. "We will need to question the four of you about the events that led up to this. I understand your young lady is in shock, so I will not push the issue today. I will just need a way to contact you so the detective that takes the case can set up interviews."

"I understand that," Troy said. "I will provide all of our information for you. We will all be living in one house once we return home, so it won't be hard to find us."

The officers entered the house and took the gunman and ringleader away as they had regained consciousness as the police entered the house. Emergency services tended to the other gunman and brought him to the ambulance. He was unconscious but would live.

Agent Stuart from the FBI walked over to Troy and his brothers, "We arrested two executives from Mid Tech. We found incriminating information that proved they were behind some illegal activities, as well as the attack on your office and homes. You can now rest easy knowing that these criminals will pay for what they have done," said Agent Stuart.

The brothers asked Agent Stuart some questions before he left but one of them always had a hand on Kiera. Her face was in a daze the entire time. Once it was just the four of them again, Eric tried to bring her back to Earth.

"Kiera," he said softly, stroking her face.

She blinked slowly as her name penetrated whatever cocoon she was hiding in. She saw the brothers' faces and began to cry. "I can't do this. It's just too much. And I don't know what this is? I just can't right now. It's too much."

Kiera left to find Agent Stuart to take her home. Troy, Jamal, and Eric looked on as Kiera got in the car with the agent.

Chapter 10: The Aftermath

Kiera awoke in her bed. She was exhausted to her core. It had been a few days since the incident. She looked around at the mess. Her life was in pieces and so was her home. She got out of the bed and started cleaning up. She wanted to get her life back together, starting with her bedroom. She picked up the little table that had fallen over and cleared away some of the clothes that lined the floor from where someone had thrown them looking for information.

After cleaning, she decided to call Jasmine. "Hey, what's going on?" Kiera asked.

"Nothing, Keke. Let's grab dinner at Cafe Deux," Jasmine responded, happy to hear from her friend.

"Okay, I will meet you there." Kiera arrived early at the cafe, arriving before Jasmine, as usual, so she grabbed a table outside. She loved the turkey avocado Panini but waited to order because she thought about trying something different tonight. Surely, Jasmine would suggest something that Kiera would enjoy just as much.

Jasmine walked into the cafe with a yellow shirt, tight blue jeggings, and heels. The men noticed her right away. They didn't notice Kiera as she was wearing jeans, a T-shirt, and a baseball cap. It wasn't her normal attire, but she wasn't in the mood for dressing up considering all she had been through,

"Hey Keke, what's going on?" asked Jasmine as she hugged Kiera before sitting down.

"Oh, everything is okay," Kiera said, trying to sound nonchalant.

"Um, I know you ain't trying to fool me, we have been friends for a long time and I know when something ain't right."

Kiera thought about it then began, "Well, I am trying to piece my life back together. My house is still a mess."

"Girl, I know," said Jasmine. "I saw the graffiti on the outside. But the inside may look better." Jasmine said, trying to pump her friend up.

Kiera gave Jasmine a little smile before continuing, "I am not sure about my job. I haven't contacted them since the incident."

"I understand," Jasmine said, "it was a tough situation. There was a bomb at the job and your house was burglarized. It's only been a few days since everything happened. Give yourself a break. You need time to get things back together."

"That's just it, I don't know how much time I need," said Kiera as she looked off in the distance.

"Kiera, what's bothering you? Is it the job or something else? Is it the guys? You didn't go into much detail about them, but I sense there is more to that conversation," said Jasmine.

"Okay, you are right. I think I have feelings for them," Kiera admitted sheepishly.

"THEM?" Jasmine exclaimed.

"Please lower your voice, everyone is looking at us! But, yes, I said them."

"So, it's true that they share women?" asked Jasmine.

"Yes, but it's not like that. We all had a connection, or so I thought. But maybe it was just fun and games for them with no serious future," Kiera said wistfully.

"Did you want more?" asked Jasmine.

"Yes, I wanted more and I thought they wanted more, but since I came back none of them have called, texted, or anything." The tears began to swell up in Kiera's eyes.

"Keke, you are a strong woman," said Jasmine, "you will get your home in order and a new job and someone else will come along and he will be just what you need. Everything will work out in its own time." Jasmine leaned across the table to hug Kiera.

"Thank you, Jazz. You're such a great friend," Kiera said, wiping the tears from her eyes. "Can we eat now and stop talking about my messed-up life? How is that fiancé of yours? How are the wedding plans coming?"

Jasmine took the not-so-subtle hint and allowed her friend to change the subject. They chatted and enjoyed the food.

***

Everything had almost returned to normal at High Technology. Troy was waiting on Jamal and Eric for their meeting; as usual. He could hear them laughing as they walked down the hall.

"What's so funny?" asked Troy in a dull tone.

"I was telling him about how the lady at Popeye's said that they didn't have any chicken when I went by there for lunch today," Jamal said. "I asked her how a chicken place can run out of chicken."

Troy, Jamal, and Eric all laughed.

"Well, let's get the meeting started," said Troy. "The renovations for the conference rooms are well on the way, and, since we were already doing repairs, we decided that we would open up the conference room and add an office," Troy continued. He was not letting his brothers interrupt him. He was all business today. "Mid Tech was up for sale and we made an offer. It was accepted this morning."

Both Jamal and Eric look excited about the purchase of Mid Tech. "Eric, would you mind going over the numbers for the purchase?" Troy asked.

Eric discussed the finances and then ceded the floor to Jamal, who discussed operations and ways to further secure High Technology from threats. The meeting ended and Troy sank down in his chair. "Has anyone called Kiera?" he asked.

"We thought you would," Jamal said.

"I'm not sure if she wants us to," said Eric quietly. "She left so fast. It was like she couldn't wait to leave us."

They looked at each other with sadness in their eyes. They had thought they had found their queen. "I know one thing," said Troy, "I can't stop thinking about her.

I have tried to stop but something inside of me is screaming that she is the one."

Eric chimed in, "When I close my eyes all I see is Kiera. When I am awake that's all I want to do is be with her."

Jamal replied, "She's always on my mind too."

"She is our queen," said Troy.

"But what should we do?" asked Eric. "I don't think she wants us or this type of relationship."

"I think she does want us. Did you see the way her body responded to all three of us? I think she was scared and ran away," said Troy.

"But how do we get her back?" asked Eric.

"We have to talk to her," said Jamal. "We have to make sure she is okay and convince her that we are the family that she needs and that we need her too."

"But what can we offer her?" asked Eric.

"We will give her the world," said Jamal. "But let's be realistic. We can offer her a home and men who will love her. We will support her and encourage her to thrive. She will want for nothing."

"But we need to make sure we are not coming on too strong," Troy said. "She needs to decide that she wants us. We cannot decide for her. I am sure she feels like she has no control over anything after the events that transpired. She deserves to control this critical aspect of her life.

***

Kiera woke the next morning to movement outside of her home. She immediately reached into her bedside table and pulled out her .38 that she purchased from a pawn shop. She was prepared for anything this time. She slowly moved toward the noise she heard coming from outside.

"Who would dare vandalize her home in broad daylight?" She moved closer to the window and the noise outside increased. She pointed the barrel of the gun at the window before coming close to see who or what it was. Kiera gasped as she saw the brothers working on her home, all bare-chested. Troy, Jamal, and Eric were painting her house.

She put the gun away in the drawer. Grabbed shorts and a white top, and went into the bathroom to freshen up before running outside. "What are you doing here?" asked Kiera.

"You needed us," said Jamal as he wiped the sweat from his forehead.

"And we need you," said Troy as he picked up the paint roller and continued to apply paint over the graffiti on the house. "Can we talk in the house, Kiera?" asked Troy as he stopped painting to look at her.

"Yes," said Kiera as she led the men into her house. She was not used to having men in her home and their large built bodies made her dining room feel tiny.

They all sat around the dining table. Troy spoke first, "Kiera, you mean a lot to us. That week was about more than protecting you. It was a way for us to show you what we had to offer and get to know you better. It might not have been ideal circumstances but it did provide us with time we would never have gotten otherwise. We want a future with you. I don't know what is about you, but my heart wants what my heart wants. I love you, Kiera. You had me from the start, and I hope you will have me and us."

Jamal spoke up next, "Baby girl, you have captured my heart. I ain't never had a woman like you. You make me a better person." I love you, baby girl.

Eric knew his brother was not a chatty guy, so he began, "Kiera, you have shown me how to be open and let others in. You are kind-hearted but bold. I love you so much. I am not the same when you aren't around. I go back to being my shy, closed-off self."

"We all want you and love you," they said in unison.

Tears welled in Kiera's eyes. She had everything she wanted right in front of her, this time she wasn't running. "I love you all too," said Kiera. "You make me the happiest woman alive. Thank you for loving and protecting me."

The tension in the air lifted. One by one, each of the brothers rose to hug her until they all embraced. Troy broke away and pulled a ring out of his pocket. He and his brothers sank to one knee.

"Will you marry us?" they asked.

"Yes," shouted Kiera, jumping up and down. She kissed each of them with long lingering kisses.

"Can we seal this engagement in the bedroom?" asked Kiera as she looked at Jamal, Eric, and Troy with hunger in her eyes.

"Lead the way, Queen," Troy said.

Epilogue

Kiera rubbed her protruding belly as she looked out the window of her house in the suburbs of Georgia. She see rabbits running through her garden filled with all kinds of flowers.

Her life had changed so much since last year. She had gotten married and had a wedding with all the bells and whistles. Now she was expecting a baby from one of her husbands. It didn't matter who the father was because she knew they would guard her and the baby with their own lives.

Troy embraced Kiera from behind. "What's on your mind sweetheart?" he asked.

"I am just happy," said Kiera. "Everything has changed so much, but I love it." Kiera's family had embraced her lifestyle after seeing how the men cared for and treated her.

"Is there anything I can bring you from the kitchen? Maybe your favorite tea?" Troy asked before releasing the embrace.

"That sounds nice. Thank you," said Kiera as she continued to gaze out the window.

As Eric passed Troy in the hallway he handed him the cup of tea, they smiled at each other. "Would you like a foot rub, darling?" he asked.

"Oh, yes," said Kiera, leaving the window to sit down next to Eric. He handed her the tea and started to massage her feet. Kiera slowly sipped the tea. "Thank you for the foot rub. My feet have been hurting all day."

"Based on the books I have been reading, they say that foot rubs are one thing that women always need during pregnancy," Eric said. Eric stayed with Kiera for a few minutes, then he left to prepare for the evening event.

Jamal found Kiera resting on the couch as he entered the living room. "Baby girl, what are you watching? Would you like some company?"

"You know I love your company," said Kiera. "But I am going to warn you that I am watching a chick flick."

"Okay," said Jamal, "I just wanted to spend time with you, it doesn't matter what we watch."

After 30 minutes, Eric and Troy came into the living room. "Kiera, we have a surprise for you. Please meet us on the patio, my love," said Troy.

Kiera got up and waddled towards the backyard. When she walked through the patio door, she heard everyone shout, "Surprise!"

Her men had thrown Kiera a baby shower. She looked around at her friends and family, and she knew she was blessed. She really had it all.

Afterwords

Thank you for reading Ours to Hold: The Brotherhood Series Book 1. I hope you enjoy this book. The series continues with Ours to Have: The Brotherhood Series book 2. Preorder at the link below.

https://www.amazon.com/dp/B094H6TN8X

NIA JOLOVE

OURS
TO HAVE

The Brotherhood
Series Book 2

Book Summary:

Jasmine, a celebrity hairstylist, and Todd a music producer are about to be married.

But before they tie the knot, they agree to a free pass week where they can be single to live out their fantasies without repercussions.

Jasmine's fantasy is to have multiple partners at once. So, she seeks out college friends Jackson, Mike, and Andre.

Jackson, Mike, and Andre have shared women before but are now looking for one woman who would love them all. Years ago, they thought Jasmine may have been the one but she left before they had a chance to explore the connection.

Will, what Jasmine shares with three men destroy what she has with Todd? Or will Todd's dark secrets end the marriage before it starts?

Lightning Source UK Ltd.
Milton Keynes UK
UKHW020309041222
413325UK00010B/641

9 798504 946085